LOVE UNEXPECTED

A FAKE RELATIONSHIP ROMANCE

ELIZA DUKE

HOT AND STEAMY ROMANCE

CONTENTS

Synopsis   v

1. Chapter One   1
2. Chapter Two   6
3. Chapter Three   12
4. Chapter Four   17
5. Chapter Five   21
6. Chapter Six   25
7. Chapter Seven   31
8. Chapter Eight   36
9. Chapter Nine   43
10. Chapter Ten   47
11. Chapter Eleven   49
12. Chapter Twelve   54

    Sign Up to Receive Free Books   61
    Preview of The Virgin's Bargain   63
    Catherine   65
    Sergei   72
    Catherine   79
    Other Books By This Author   86

Copyright   89

Made in "The United States" by:

Eliza Duke

© Copyright 2020 – Eliza Duke

ISBN: 978-1-64808-070-8

ALL RIGHTS RESERVED. No part of this publication may be reproduced or transmitted in any form whatsoever, electronic, or mechanical, including photocopying, recording, or by any informational storage or retrieval system without express written, dated and signed permission from the author

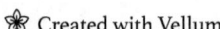 Created with Vellum

SYNOPSIS

Nakita had no idea what she was getting into, when she accepted an acting job pretending to be the girlfriend of famous golfer, Eric Vanlare. From their first encounter, she realized he was going to be a handful. He was stunningly handsome and she knew he had amazing hands. She felt out of her depth, inexperienced in love and still a virgin. What seemed like an easy job was going to be more than she had bargained for. Could she concentrate on the job at hand while falling for such a handsome golfer?

CHAPTER ONE

ERIC

Thumping beats pulsed throughout the new club. The intensity of the music created an electrifying motion of energy that could be felt all over. As I looked around, at all the hot bodies, I felt alive. This was certainly the place to be if you wanted to be surrounded by plenty of gorgeous women gyrating all over the floor. I looked over at Matthew, my best friend and winked.

"Pretty cool party, uh?" He yelled over the crowd.

"Yeah, this is awesome," I yelled back.

I was happy to have Matthew by my side that night; he was the guy that could cheer me up , no matter how down I felt. Our friendship went as far back as high school and I could depend on him always, no matter what. He used to be on the golf circuit, but his career took a tumble when he tore his rotator cuff a few years back. We had been playing together all through high school and college. The fact that he couldn't play golf had totally devastated him.. He hadn't let it get him down though; he wasn't the kind of guy that would fall into a depression. He was always laughing, the life of the party and in general, his outlook was always positive.

These days Matthew worked for me. He didn't want to give up on golf. He'd made it his personal mission to make sure that I got to the Masters and he'd succeeded. It was awesome to have a friend like that behind you every step of the way. What more could I ask for? He had agreed to work as my caddie, and having him on the courses with me was beyond what I could ever hope for with regards to a support system. It was certainly more than my father did, though I couldn't discredit the money he'd put into making sure I was a success.

I smiled as a few girls approached our booth and asked if they could come in. We had a private area with bottle service and people had been in and out all night. As the girls started chatting among themselves, Matthew started pouring them some drinks. He looked over at me and I nodded for him to make me another.

"So, your father was harsh with you today?"

"It wasn't him being harsh as much as making it obvious that he didn't want me embarrassing him again on this tour." I said indignantly.

Matthew laughed, "He acts like you do these things on purpose to aggravate him."

"Yeah, I know. Believe me, I want to win more than anything."

"You will buddy, trust me. I have your back and you're going all the way this time. So, what was his whole deal anyways?"

I shook my head, "You wouldn't believe it if I told you."

"Try me."

"He wants me to get a girlfriend. A fake one, and pretend that I'm settling down. He said that I've embarrassed him too much with my 'playboy, party ways,' and that he's cutting me off if I don't do as he says."

"Holy shit man, what are you going to do?"

I frowned, "I'm going to do whatever he wants. I can't get cut off from money man, and it's just until the Masters are over. I just have to put up with him and what he says until then. Apparently, they are bringing in some unknown actress to play my girlfriend."

Matthew laughed, "Are you serious?"

"Yeah, ridiculous, uh."

"Wow, your dad doesn't mess around."

"Nope. So, this is probably going to be my last night as a single guy until the tour is over."

"Well, we better start enjoying ourselves," Matthew said laughing.

As the bottles kept coming, our eyes glazed over from intoxication, and girls came in and out all night long. They were all so beautiful. While on the dance floor I was feeling so free. My feet felt light and the music coursed through my veins. In front of me danced a pretty blonde. She started to unbutton my shirt and I moved my gyrating body closer to her. She was hotter than hell and she had a huge smile on her face.

Miss Blondie and I began sexually tangoing on the dance floor and eventually left the club lip-locked. Several minutes and a taxi ride later, we drunkenly stepped into my apartment. It was a luxury apartment that my father paid for and it was a total chick magnet. Black leather, high tech entertainment, all the amenities of riches with a killer view. She oohed and aahed all over the apartment before I pulled her close to me.

Wrapping my arms around her hot curvy body, I pulled her into me, kissing her aggressively. Our tongues met with fierceness. Her reaction wasn't surprising. She giggled under her breath and I realized she might be thinking we'd be an item after this. They all thought that way. I had a reputation for being a lady's man. She kissed like a freight train though and it made me think of other naughtier things she could do with her mouth. Our tongues were teasing each other and we started ripping clothes off in a heightened fashion. We made a trail of clothing all the way to the bedroom. We started stripping. Her suckle breasts drew me in and I naturally licked using the tip of my tongue invoking a whimpering moan. Her youth showed as she giggled and shivered from anxious energy. She was quite a looker. My body responded instantly. My stylish pants bulging from the throbbing intensity.

I KISSED her again and she eagerly twisted and sucked on my tongue. She was driving me mad and holding back was getting incredibly difficult.

"I want you, Eric," she said with clenched teeth, breathing deeply.

That much was obvious and I was about to give her exactly what she wanted. Her hands caressed my chest, while I took the rest of my clothes off , and then she slid her hands down between my thighs. I looked at her with wanting eyes. She begun to lick my navel. My body trembled and hardened and I led her where I truly wanted her. The edge of her tongue swirling and circling my tip, throwing me into a bodily convulsion. I couldn't help but groan loudly with delight. Even though her seemingly innocent giggles earlier demonstrated her youth; she knew exactly how to massage me into a blissful state. I put my fingers through her silky soft hair and moaned while she satisfied my desire. I wanted to fill her and feel her tighten around me. I gently placed my hands under her chin, moving her upward. This was a surprise to her, but soon she'd feel the surprise of her life.

"Lay back sweetheart," I said breathlessly.

She smiled that beautiful smile and I placed my body on top of her. I could feel the smoothness of her breasts touch my pecs. The throbbing intensified as I slid myself deep inside her. She wrapped her legs around my hips, pulling me closer and the moisture enveloped me. I loved the way she felt. Her warmth was intoxicating. I couldn't get enough of that feeling. Women were incredible beings; they provided so much pleasure. She moaned my name as I thrust smoothly back and forth. With every thrust, I went deeper building up the intensity between us. She moved her legs around my waist as I penetrated her with ferocity.

She was loud and she made it well known how much she was enjoying herself. I smiled down at her, happy that I was bringing her pleasure. There was nothing like looking into a girl's eyes when she was in ecstasy; every thrust brought about more emotions. My body was on the verge, but I was holding back to allow her to climax first. I wanted to explode inside her the moment she was ready. I could tell by her face and her screaming that she had to be close to sharing in our mutual euphoria. I thrust and she cried out. That was it for me. My body jerked with excited release. The buildup was massive and seconds later, I groaned, surrendering my essence into her. I collapsed on her chest and heard that familiar, not so innocent now, giggle again.

CHAPTER TWO

NIKITA

It was Friday night and I was hoping to forget my crushed dreams for the time being. It was just one of those days that I needed to learn to get over and let loose for a little while. I tried making light of the situation, but when it came right down to it, I was devastated that I didn't get the role on the reality show I'd auditioned for. It would have meant everything for my career. For most people, a reality show is nothing special, but for me it would have been a beginning. It was the exposure I needed. What was I thinking quitting school though? The last thing I needed was to prove my parents right. I'd never hear the end of it and that alone was enough to send fear flooding through my veins. I wanted to be a movie star; it was something that I had dreamed of my whole life. I remember at around 5 years old, taking a candlestick, as though it was an Oscar, and standing in front of our little coffee table giving my acceptance speech. My parents knew I wanted to be an actress from that day forward.

I stared at myself in the mirror; noticing the layers of my long brown hair curled around my shoulders. I looked hard into those emerald green hued eyes staring back at me, attempting to change the desperately saddened look into something more positive. People say, 'fake it 'til you make', but wow that was hard to swallow when things weren't going as planned.

"You look great," my sister Mandy said as she peeked her head into the bathroom door.

I smiled at my sister and then looked down at myself. I was wearing a tight red dress that hugged my every curve in all the right ways.

"Thanks, you don't look so bad yourself."

We were planning on going out for dinner and drinks; it was exactly what I needed to get my mind off everything. My sister was always very supportive of my career and I wasn't sure what I would have done without her. Our parents lived in Europe and when I chose to leave, I took Mandy with me. Mandy jumped at the opportunity and considering her job she could work anywhere. Mandy was a freelance writer, which gave her amazing flexibility to work anywhere.

Although we shared the same emerald eyes and brown hair, we didn't look much alike. She took after our father and I more resembled our mother. Her eyes were a bit smaller with shorter lashes, her nose a bit longer, and her lips were a tad thinner. She was still a beauty, but not quite the Hollywood type.

"Let's get going; you're taking forever in there," Mandy said impatiently.

"Well, excuse me, I'm trying not to fall into a depression in here," I said half-joking and half-serious.

"Oh get over yourself, let's get to it."

The great thing about having Mandy as a sister was her straightforward nature. She'd never let me stew in self-pity for very long.

We strolled into the restaurant chatting it up and were

seated rather quickly. As we feasted on an array of appetizers from the local Kelsey's, I started to feel like myself again for the first time all day. I couldn't believe the day I had had, but considering Mandy was with me things were starting to look up.

"Maybe you should start dating someone to get your mind off things."

I laughed, "What are you talking about? That's the last thing I need to do. I don't have the time or the patience. I need to focus on my career, because right now it's falling apart."

"Oh c'mon! It's not that bad. Plus, you'd have probably hated being on reality TV anyways. Just focus on TV and movies for now. Look at Kim Kardashian, do you really want to walk in the footsteps of that train wreck?"

I laughed and then said, "No, that wasn't really my goal, but the thing is, it would have allowed me some exposure and that has certainly launched a few careers," I winked.

"Uh, yeah, who needs it," saying with a fry in hand and a cavalier expression.

She was probably right. As much as I loved the idea of being an actress, reality TV would have completely forced me out of my comfort zone. I guess I just wanted it all too much. Jillian, my trusted agent, was working on new gigs as we spoke and for all I knew I'd be getting a call tomorrow for a new gig, a better gig than the last one.

Just then my phone rang and it showed that it was Jillian. Oh, thank goodness, I hoped she has good news for me.

"Hello," I said with an eager and somewhat chill faking voice.

"Nakita, it's Jillian."

"Oh Jillian, I was just thinking about you, you must have ESP. What's up? Do you have anything good for me?" I had my fingers crossed with anticipation of a possible audition.

"We need to talk. I'd like us to meet for coffee and talk, sooner rather than later?" Her voice sounded rushed and intriguing. I thought this could be promising, but I wasn't quite sure.

I decided to invite her to Kelsey's so we could talk right then. It wasn't long before she arrived at the restaurant and she sat down with a smile on her face.

Jillian adjusted her glasses before saying, "I'm glad this could happen so quickly."

"Yeah, of course. I've been hoping and wanting good news after such a disappointing day."

"Well, I guess that depends on your definition of 'good.'" The quirky smile on her face made me wonder what she was about to offer me.

I laughed, "Great, I can't wait to hear about it."

"Okay, so here it is. I got an interesting call last night and it might be something you would be interested in, but it is unusual. This gig is the first of its kind I've come across."

I nodded, nervously. "Well, let me hear it and we'll go from there."

"Alright." She pulled out her day planner where she had some notes jotted down. After scanning the notes she looked up at me.

"Okay, so here's the deal. There is a pro-golfer in Miami, that is, believe it or not, looking for a fake girlfriend for three months."

"What? That's crazy. What does that even mean? I'm not a hooker for crying out loud, Jillian!" I started feeling anxiety build up. Was this what it was coming down to, I was going to have to take gigs as an escort until I got my big break.

Jillian adjusted her glasses showing her own nervousness, "Hey relax. That's not what I'm talking about here; it's nothing like that. He's not looking for sex. It's an acting job, strictly acting. He basically wants a trophy girlfriend, someone to put on his arm, have pictures taken with, parade around with. It's all a façade, he just needs it to appear as if he has a girlfriend."

I couldn't believe what I was hearing. "Are you sure? You are confident that it has nothing to do with sex, that there are no expectations?" I looked at Mandy and she had a wide grin on her face.

"Absolutely not. I made sure of that when I discussed things with him. He is strictly looking for an actress, someone who can play a role properly, and you can certainly do that."

"Three months in Miami? I guess it could be worse."

"Nope, it's quite hot and mostly sunny days there. You will love it. Not to mention as his girlfriend he will probably wine and dine you quite lavishly."

I nodded, my interest piqued, "How much does it pay?"

She slowly and deliberating said in a higher than usual voice, "Fifty thousand dollars for three months."

My jaw hit the floor. "Holy shit, that's fantastic news." I couldn't believe what I was hearing. "Holy shit."

"I thought you might like that. Money is no object to this guy and I know you can use the money," she said enthusiastically.

"Okay, who is he? I don't know the first thing about golf." My head was whirling with excitement and an overwhelming feeling I couldn't pinpoint.

"Eric Vanlare."

Mandy responded, "Yes, I've definitely heard of him. He's a real player, in more than one sense."

"Yes, well apparently, his father threatened to take his money away if he didn't clean his act up until the Masters were over."

I looked to Mandy, "What should I do?"

"You're obviously going to take it. This could open a lot of doors. You're going to be photographed with someone famous." It was slowly sinking in and I knew this could turn out to be an opportunity of a lifetime.

I turned back to Jillian. "Okay, let's do this."

3
CHAPTER THREE
NAKITA

It was Saturday and I was flying to Miami on United, first class. I couldn't help but think to myself, you're so crazy, Nakita. A girlfriend to a famous golfer for three months, what in the hell are you getting yourself into. It was all a little insane, but it was also really exciting. When the plane touched down, the butterflies in my stomach went into my throat. I quickly grabbed my carry-on, hurrying off the plane. I couldn't believe how nervous I was.

As I exited the gate I saw a handsome gentleman waiting for me. I knew right away that it wasn't Eric since I had already seen him on video. He was obviously someone important, he carried himself with total confidence and was definitely in charge.

He held out his hand as I walked up to him. I took it and he shook with a firmness that confirmed his character. "Hi, Nakita, I presume? I'm Matthew. I'm Eric's best friend, he asked me to come and pick you up." he said unapologetically.

"Well, it's nice to meet you Matthew. Thanks for picking me up," I said with a nervous giggle. Were all the men in this Sunny State that handsome? First Eric, and now Matthew.

Matthew led her towards a luxurious black Lexus. She could

see the all leather interior and it had obviously been washed and waxed recently. He took her bag and opened the front passenger door in a gentlemanly fashion. Sliding into the cushiony soft leather, Nakita felt herself momentarily relaxing.

"We are heading to Eric's home. You will love it there, it's quite beautiful. The estate is well taken care of."

I just nodded, trying to take it all in. I was so nervous to meet Eric and I wasn't sure how it was all going to work.

When we pulled up to the estate, I couldn't believe my eyes. The house, which was more like a mansion was situated overlooking the ocean. The property was vast and lusciously green. The ocean waves could be heard crashing against the shoreline. It was heavenly. Who lived like this? As we rounded the driveway, I noticed the exquisite nature of the front door. Everything was designed perfectly, creating an air of wealth. I tried to shake off the intimidation that I was feeling being in the midst of such affluence and the kind of people I knew I was going to meet.

Matthew came around and opened the door for me in his courteous fashion. I stepped onto the brick layered driveway and followed slowly behind looking all around. As we entered the house, I became overwhelmed seeing the marble floors, lavish furnishings, and incredible artwork hanging from the walls. He brought me into the study where Eric was sitting behind a mahogany desk. He smiled and immediately got up to walk towards me. I was taken aback by the magnitude of his good looks. His body was chiseled, which was well-defined by his fitted grey polo shirt. Photos didn't do him the justice he deserved. His face was distinguished and incredibly handsome. He had big eyes with thick dark eyelashes, a refined nose, and full lips.

"Nakita, it's a pleasure to meet you. I am so happy to have you come all this way. It must be quite the unusual gig for you," Eric said with a cheerfulness and just a hint of sarcasm.

I grinned and chuckled, "Yes, I have to say I was a little surprised, but also intrigued, as well."

"Good. I just want to say first off I have no interest in having a real girlfriend."

I laughed and then responded sarcastically, "Obviously, that would be why you hired someone to play this part."

Matthew swallowed hard and slightly chuckled, "She got you there, buddy. You're cute Nakita. You will have to keep on your toes with this one."

"Yeah, I guess she told you," Eric started laughing. "I just wanted to make sure things were clear, this is a very unusual situation after all. Even having a fake girlfriend is a whole new experience for me."

"It's no problem. I totally understand."

He smiled and I felt almost faint. It was important to keep my cool though. He had already made things clear, this was to all be an act.

"Let me show you around the property."

"Of course, I'd love to see." I followed him out of the study, walking through a beautifully decorated hallway, and a huge kitchen with an entrance onto the patio. The patio had a large entertainment area with a below ground pool and a sweet gazebo next to it. When you looked outward, the landscaped property went out practically to the ocean front. It was absolutely astonishing. The three of us stopped and sat on the cushioned patio chairs to admire the view. I could definitely get used to this, I thought to myself.

Eric looked over at me and smiled. "So, Nakita you will be living here with me," He asked in a somewhat rhetorical manner.

"Sure, thank you," I said. Of course, I wasn't going to deny an invitation to stay in such a heavenly place.

"We'll put you up in an excellent Airbnb for a few weeks and then we'll set you up here after we officially meet at my favorite club. That will technically be the first time we meet. I will, of course, be behaving myself since that's what I do these days," Eric said jokingly and then laughed.

MATTHEW WAS LOVING every minute of this meeting. It was pretty obvious that Eric and Matthew were close, after all, he was sitting in on a pretty important meeting.

"I will expect you to come on to me Nakita if you think you can handle that." Eric winked at Matthew.

I smiled, "I'm a great actress. Flirting is easy."

"Great."

"So, when is this epic night supposed to be happening?" Matthew interjected.

"Tonight. I would like to get on with things if you know what I mean," Eric said while starting to fidget in his seat getting seemingly restless.

"Okay, I'm in," I said excited by the prospect of standing next to such a hot, rich, and what seemed to be, charming man.

He nodded with a smile. "You won't regret this Nakita. You are going to have the time of your life."

"Well, you might regret this Nakita, but he's not wrong about having the time of your life," Matthew added, with a big grin.

I laughed, "Okay, great."

"You will see a lot of Matthew as well, he is my right-hand man and when I'm working he is my caddy, so we are around each other quite a bit."

"Okay, that's not a problem." Two stunningly gorgeous men by my side, nope, no complaints there I thought to myself.

"Good, he will always be keeping an eye on you, so you don't need to worry about being in a situation that isn't safe for you."

I smiled, "Well, I certainly appreciate that."

"It will be my pleasure Nakita." He winked at me. Oh, I was going to have quite a handful with these two, I could already tell.

"Well, I'm looking forward to working with you guys. It wasn't a job that I expected to ever come up, but it is one that will keep me working until the next gig so I appreciate the chance. I think it's going to be a great opportunity and a lot of fun. I have never been to Miami."

"You will love it here," They both said in unison.

The two guys started making plans while I listened in. My heart was beating a mile a minute, I couldn't believe it was all going down that night. I was cool with it, it was just all happening so fast.

When Eric looked over at me and smiled again, my heart started beating fast again. He was so hot that it was hard to look right at him. It was like looking at the sun. Matthew was going to bring me to an Airbnb that day to get settled in and then I would start to prepare my role for that evening. It had to look authentic and it had to appear as if I was the one hitting on him. He already had a terrible reputation for being a playboy. We all got up to leave and I couldn't wipe the grin off my face even if I'd wanted to.

4

CHAPTER FOUR

ERIC

We could not keep our eyes off Hailey the whole time we were interviewing her, she was gorgeous. When she made jokes, there was a glimmer in her eyes that was intoxicating, it made me want to know more about her. The picture they gave us didn't do her justice, sure I thought she was pretty, but meeting her in person put her on a whole new level. She was incredible, she was beautiful, intelligent, and joked around like some of my guy friends. She had no problem telling it like it was, which was refreshing to see from a girl. This was certainly going to be interesting.

Matthew and I were at the same club that we hit up the night I had fun with Miss Blondie. Not only was it an awesome place, but I wanted to come back with a cleaner reputation so that people would stop talking about me. We got our regular booth and the girls started hitting on us immediately.

"Under Armour shouldn't be just sponsoring you, they should be hiring you to be an underwear model," A pretty blonde said.

I laughed, "Right? That's what I thought."

The girl laughed, "What took you so long to come back to the club. We've all missed you."

"Well, I needed to lay low for a while. Make everyone happy."

I smiled at her and she was eating it right up. It wasn't hard when she was making it so easy. I could have told her just about anything. She wasn't really interested in me, but my status and fame. I glanced around the room to see if I spotted Nakita, but it didn't seem like she'd arrived yet.

A few of my friends came up to the booth and we shook hands. I asked, "How you guys doing tonight?"

"Great, just blowing off some steam, you know how it is. Are you ready for the Masters?"

"As ready as I'm going to be. I'm looking forward to getting started, should be awesome."

"No kidding." His friend stated.

"Excuse me?"

Both my friends and I turned around to find Nakita standing there. She was dressed in a red skin-tight strapless dress, black heels, and she was breathtaking. Her brown hair was curled over her shoulders and her bright emerald eyes just lit the entire room. She was the most beautiful woman in there, hands down and the way she was smiling at me hinted a bit of sensuality. She came across as ultra-confident and probably could have had any man in the room. I glanced at my friend and judging by the look on his face he was sizing her up for himself.

"Yes?" I said before he could.

"I was wondering if you would mind if I joined you. I could use a drink if you're pouring them," she spoke over the music, but with a sexy sultry tone that was noticed by both of us.

I grinned, "Absolutely, the more, the merrier," I said, forgetting the fact that I had a girl beside me already. I heard a gasp next me and glanced at the blonde. "Let's make room for the lady to sit down, please." We both shifted down to allow Nakita to sit alongside me. The blonde was immediately pissed and got up to leave without another word.

Nakita sat down and there wasn't even a look of recognition on her face when she looked back at me. She was really playing it cool and I loved it.

"I'm Nakita, my friend ditched me for a guy," she said with halfhearted relief, "So I need a new friend. Can you help me with that?" Raising one eyebrow in a very seductive coy fashion.

She was being very charming and I almost wished that it was real. "I think I could." I glanced at my friend, "I'll catch you later man."

"Sure." He walked away looking disappointed.

I turned back to Nakita, "Let me grab you a drink." I quickly mixed her up a cocktail and handed it to her. She took a few tentative sips, her eyes never leaving mine.

"Thanks. So, do you have a name?" She said convincingly.

I laughed, "I'm Eric Vanlare."

"It's nice to meet you."

"What do you say we do a little dancing?"

She smiled that stunning smile at me. "I would love that."

We got up and made our way to the dance floor which was packed with hot bodies and blaring music moving the crowd. We started dancing very close together, our bodies getting into a rhythm. She was acting the part of a flirty girl who wanted to take a man home. I couldn't help but respond to her, in fact, she was turning me on in ways that I didn't expect. She turned around and started gyrating against me. She was incredibly sexy. I could have easily put my hands on her ass in the same way I had done with a hundred women before her. I had to snap myself out of the spell though. I was acting a little too much like my old self, getting too close to her. It was easy to get drawn in and lose yourself in this girl. She was amazing and she could turn me on as quickly as flipping a switch.

The way she was moving I wondered if things would progress past this into the evening. I shook the thoughts off immediately and tried to remember that she was playing a part. She was no more interested in me than she was in anyone else in that room. If she was coming on to me, it was just an act. But she was a damn good actress, because I was completely captivated by her. My body was reacting in a way that could get me in such trouble. I needed to keep my cool and remember that we were both acting until the Masters were over and then she would return home. It was no big deal, I could totally handle the situation. But when she turned around and smiled up at me I wasn't sure I believed what I was telling myself.

CHAPTER FIVE
NAKITA

The next day I got a call from Eric telling me to meet him in the lobby of the Airbnb luxury building I was staying at. He said we were going to the beach. It would be our first official day of being a couple in public. I pulled out a hot pink bikini and a sexy looking wrap to go along with it. I was glad that I had brought the cutest sandals to match. It was a great outfit that showed off all my best features. I slipped into it quickly, thankful that I had waxed earlier that week. One less thing to worry about. I looked in the mirror and touched up my waterproof makeup and pulled my hair up in a pink and black clip. I tied the wrap around my waist and slipped into my sandals. I was all ready to go and looking forward to a glass of Champagne. I hurried out of the room and headed downstairs.

I found Eric sitting on a sofa drinking coffee when I arrived. Well, the rich certainly are well taken care of I thought amusingly.

"Hi, I'm ready," I said while flaunting all my sexy curves to drive him a bit crazy.

He looked up and smiled at me approvingly. "You look fantastic, Nakita."

"Why, thank you. What do you plan on wearing to the beach?"

"Oh don't worry about me. I'm covered."

We went back outside to the car and I put my beach bag in the backseat. He got inside as well and smiled at me. He was so handsome that I found it hard to breathe at times. It wasn't a long drive to the beach and when we got there, I almost burst out laughing. I assumed that we were going to grab a couple of lawn chairs and sit on the beach, what I didn't expect was to find a beautiful beach house.

"Wow."

"Don't get too excited; it's not mine. It's my father's, but why not go to the beach in style, right?" He said in his usual charming way. This was the most majestic beach house I had ever seen. The walkway was surrounded by beautiful flowers and plants. We walked into the foyer that had an exotic fish tank that was centered in the midst of marble walled fountains. Everything was so breathtaking I was captured by the ambiance. Off the sitting room was a massive patio that had an incredibly shaped pool and Jacuzzi with a set of steps leading onto the beach.

"I'm going to go change. Make yourself at home. There should be some Champagne in the fridge, if you don't mind, you can put it on ice."

"Yeah, sure thing."

As I watched him leave the room, I spun around in awe of everything. What a life. I made my way to the kitchen and opened the fridge to find it fully stocked. I grabbed a bottle of Champagne and found a bucket for the ice. While filling the bucket, I noticed the intricate detail of the splash-back, which looked hand carved. Then I carried everything outside and sat with my legs crossed letting the warm of the sun wash over me. Suddenly, realizing I hadn't put sunscreen on, I grabbed my

Macy's beach bag and pulled out Hawaiian Tropic. I lathered my skin to ensure an even tan. I had to look my best for Eric and all his cronies. I was just finishing up when Eric came outside. He was shirtless. I immediately noticed his rip six-pack covered with curly soft sexy chest hair and his bulging biceps. You could tell he spent a lot of time in the gym and I was going to appreciate the view.

"Do you need some help with that?" he asked, while watching me apply the sunscreen to my nicely shaven legs.

"You can do my back if you don't mind. I can never get it," I said with an innocent sounding voice.

"Sure." He grabbed the bottle and I turned around. He squirted the sunscreen onto his hands and then started rubbing it into my back. The feeling of his hands made me flinch and the coolness of the sunscreen gave me goosebumps. It always felt cooler when someone else applied it. I felt a bit awkward having him put the sunscreen on, but it brought a smile to my face nonetheless. His hands were strong and I felt like I was getting a massage from a masseuse. He took his time and made sure every inch of me was covered.

"Thank you," I said, for more than just the application, I thought.

"No problem. It was my pleasure," Eric said in a somewhat flirty manner.

I turned around and took the bottle from him. "Do you need some?"

"I took care of that when I was changing, but thanks." I felt slightly let down by that response, but it was probably for the best.

He went to the bucket and pulled out the Champagne. He pointed it in the direction of the water and popped the cork.

"Oh, I forgot glasses!" I said embarrassed.

He chuckled, "No problem, let me get them." He went back

inside and returned with two flutes. He proceeded to pour us both a glass of Champagne and handed me one. I took a sip and sighed. It was the most delicious Champagne I had ever tasted.

"Wow!"

"That good, is it?"

I giggled, "Yes, oh my goodness. Thank you. The intense flavors can overwhelm the senses."

"I'm glad that you like it."

Sitting out there with him was truly relaxing and I was glad that I had agreed to it. The beach entertained the most prominent individuals, their families and friends. It was a beautiful day with the sun beating down on us. The sounds of the ocean filled the air. I leaned back in the lounge chair, enjoying the company and the impeccable Champagne. We enjoyed chatting and getting to know one another. After several glasses of bubbly my mind felt a little heavy. The buzz didn't ruin the ability to savor every aspect of that beautiful day. At one point, he asked me if I wanted to go for a dip. He grabbed my hand and we went down the steps onto the beach. The sand was hot beneath my feet and I ran straight into the ocean.

A few people recognized Eric and came running up to him. They got pictures with him on their phones and it was obvious that they were taking pictures of us while we were in the water together. I was sure we would see some social media posts the next day, we might even find ourselves on the cover of a magazine. I felt both excited and nervous all at the same time. Things were starting to get interesting.

CHAPTER SIX
ERIC

We were in the water cooling off from the hot day and I couldn't stop looking at Nakita. She was so hot in the pink bikini. Her stomach was flat and toned and her full breasts were practically calling to me. I couldn't stop staring at her round ass, which her bikini bottoms were hugging nicely. She was incredibly sexy, especially when she laughed and she laughed a lot. All I wanted to do was pull her into my arms and never let her go. How did I get so lucky that this beautiful girl was going to be in my company for a few months?

I kept having to remind myself that it was all just pretend, but she was a great person to pretend with, that's for sure. I wasn't the only one checking her out either. She was being noticed way more than me today, which made me feel a little uncomfortable. They were probably wondering if she was some kind of celebrity that they didn't recognize. Where had I plucked this new girl from? The questions were most likely circulating on social media sites. Who was that mysterious girl hanging out with Eric Vanlare? Thankfully she was there with me and couldn't be taken away. Her cheeks were flushed from the sun or maybe it was the Champagne, but she had never looked more beautiful.

I moved closer to her and put my arm around her pulling her close. She smiled up at me. It was the perfect scene for photos. Two lovers out in the water, embracing each other. I couldn't have planned it better if I had tried. The water was cold, so it felt nice having our warm bodies close together. She wrapped her arms around my waist and hugged me closer.

"Are you having a good time." I ask looking deeply into her radiant emeralds, which sparkled brightly in the sunshine.

"The best, what an awesome day. Thank you," She said, as the waves gently rolled over our shoulders as we bobbed in the water.

"Do you want to go in and dry off?"

"Yes, I do. Maybe we can have another glass of Champagne." I was thoroughly enjoying spoiling her with my riches.

"Sure, anything you want. I can grill us up some dinner too if you'd like."

"That would be great, I should probably eat something with all this Champagne."

I laughed, "No problem. Let's go in."

We started walking back along the beach and she slipped her feet back into her stylish sandals. I noticed people staring at us and taking pictures, so I pulled her close for a hug and squeezed her tight. She giggled and embraced me convincingly, we were supposed to be lovers, after all. It felt good to hold her close and warm her skin that had cooled from the water. Camera clicks continued and I played it as casual as possible. There were times when it felt awkward to be that close to her, I barely knew her and this was a scene that was more romantic than sexual. Nakita naturally attracted attention in all the right ways, which would help rebuild my personal brand. The new me, a handsome gentleman and taken.

A girl approached us and asked for my autograph. I let go of Nakita and she turned and smiled at the girl. She was completely sweet and gracious as a few people approached us to talk. I couldn't have asked for a better opportunity to show her off to everyone. As I signed autographs one girl piped up and asked, "Are you guys dating?"

I smiled, "This is my girl, Nakita. So, you'll be seeing a lot more of her around. I was looking for better and I've found it."

"Awww."

I laughed, "My goal right now is winning the Masters. It's going to be a hell of a year." There was clapping as the crowd before us got bigger. Everyone had their phones out and I wasn't sure who was taking pictures and who was recording video.

Nakita looked up at me and smiled, just the way a girlfriend would who was proud of her man. I grinned down at her looking forward to sitting on the patio with her and making some dinner. There was no doubt we would be gracing the front covers of magazines the next day for sure.

There were a few squeals and they asked if they could take pictures of us together. Nakita agreed and we posed like the good couple we were pretending to be. These impromptu photo opts hopefully would get my father off my back for a while, dealing with him could be so exhausting at times.

"She's so pretty," One bystander said.

"Awe, thank you," Nakita said smiling warmheartedly.

"Well, we have to get going. I've promised my girl that I would make her some dinner."

As they walked away, I took Nakita's hand in mine and we made our way up the steps and journeyed back to the luxurious outside entertainment area. I turned, waving to my fans and they returned the wave, calling out that they loved me. Receiving such adoration was great for the ego.

As we ventured over to the table, Nakita laughed and said,

"Wow, that was intense. So, that's your life, uh? Talk about a little crazy."

"Yeah, well, sometimes. You might want to get used to that if you continue your acting career."

She smiled, "I suppose, you're right." She seemed lost in thought. She didn't talk much about her career and I didn't want to pry. I was surprised she hadn't made some kind of name for herself. She was definitely a Hollywood beauty and her acting skill was impressive.

"Have a seat. I'm going to get another bottle of Champagne and get the grill heated."

"Thanks."

I poured us both another glass of Champagne and handed it to her, I was tempted to lean in and kiss her, but I knew it wasn't the right time and I didn't know how she'd react. Timing is everything. I walked back in the house to gather the ingredients for grilling.

"Everything okay in there?"

"Yes, I just got some chicken and vegetables together."

"Oh cool. Do you need any help?"

I smiled, "No, I have things under control, thanks."

She nodded and looked out at the water. I had never seen her looking more at peace and genuinely happy than she did right at that moment. She was beautiful in any light, but right then she was positively stunning. I sat down beside her and sipped the best Champagne money could buy.

"I just want to thank you for being here," I said with overflowing gratitude.

She looked at me in surprise.

"I mean, I know this is a job for you, but I think you are doing a fantastic job and I just want to thank you."

She grinned, "It's no problem. I'm having a great time, so it makes the job even easier. I'm glad to have this opportunity. It's all very exciting for me."

"Great, I'm glad it's not torture for you." I said with a hint of sarcasm.

"Of course not."

"Do you want to go have a few drinks later, after we eat."

She giggled, "I guess we will have to see how I feel after this. I don't normally drink this much. I don't want to be too tipsy in public."

I laughed, "I guess we have been drinking all day. How about we hit up a restaurant and have coffee and dessert instead?"

She smiled, "That sounds perfect actually, let's do that. Are you sure you don't just want to stay here?"

"No, let's go out in public. That's what we're doing together after all, isn't it?"

"Sure no problem, whatever you want. You're the boss."

I frowned slightly. Yes, that was true. There was nothing more between us than that. I could live with that, I supposed, it really wasn't a big deal. I just wanted us seen as much as possible so that the word would get out fast that I was making changes and had a girl in my life. Once that happened people's opinions of me would start to change and that was what I wanted and needed most of all.

I started grilling the chicken and glazed it with a mild BBQ sauce. The breeze caught the aroma, filling the air, which captured the attention of both of us. The vegetables were sautéed in a separate container with spices and olive oil on them. Though this was a quick meal, I knew she'd love it. Everything looked and smelled delicious. I served our dinner on handmade ceramic plates I had received from a devoted fan, they had been handmade in Thailand.

"This looks great. A chef in the making. Ooh, pretty design," She noticed the carvings immediately.

I laughed, "Hey, what can I say. I try. They were given as a gift and they're handcrafted, made in Bangkok, incredible, uh."

She smiled joyfully as we ate. Her smile was contagious and I had a permanent grin throughout dinner. I started to formulate a plan for the evening. Word had probably gotten out, so there was no need to do anything crazy, but maybe crazy was what we needed. A devilish smile crossed my face.

CHAPTER SEVEN
ERIC

A few days later, we entered the club and went to the private patio with the amazing over-sized grills. The music pulsated inside, projecting out for us to still enjoy the beats. I saw that Hailey was talking with Matt. Matt had arrived with a few friends and everyone was gathering on bar stools around a few high tables. Matt and I never had that much fun with girls before and we usually wanted to rid ourselves of them shortly after our needs were met. But the scene on the terrace was unique, because everyone got along as if they had been friends forever.

Nakita and I were starting to become friends, which made things feel more comfortable and less contrived. In fact, it almost felt like we were really dating, imagine that. That made the situation a lot better for both of us.

Matt was at the grill cooking up some delicious steaks while another girl was making salad. The distinctive smells in the air were unimaginable and it was nice to have everyone together for a meal. We all fit together quite nicely. Nakita offered to get everyone another beer, which would be my first for the evening.

Whether drinking or not, I always knew how to have fun and chat it up.

"How can I help?" I asked.

"Oh, you don't worry about anything old man, we wouldn't want you to pull anything," Matt said humorously. I wasn't old, but I was getting older as a golfer and I needed this win. I had momentarily taken rest on a nearby leather lounge chair, but it turned into more than a minute.

I laughed, "Easy there, big guy. It was just a nap. I had a roaring headache and it hit me fast. I didn't want to be a party pooper all night so I just needed to close my eyes for a sec."

"Yeah, yeah," Matt said mockingly.

I sat down beside Nakita, brushing my hand against the side of her thigh, initiating a little wiggle, and toasted a cheer with her. The night was going to be fun and possibly surprising. As it begun, I inhaled carefree and relaxing feelings.

Matt finished up on the grill and he plated the steaks. Another girl, Sabrina added baked potatoes and a bowl of salad on the side. The meal looked sinful and my stomach growled. I cut into the steak and it was juicy and tender, just as I liked it. Matt was a genius chef especially with grilling; you wouldn't want anyone else cooking a steak for you.

"This is fantastic. You guys did an excellent job," Nakita said while savoring every bite she ate.

"I agree," everyone said in harmony.

"Well, thank you. I will cook steaks any day for the future champion," Matt boasted with confidence as though the win was already mine.

I smiled. "That's what I like to hear."

We all chatted among ourselves, mainly about the tournament, and what there was to do in Miami. Miami had a Latin flare that could get anyone dancing and eating all the spice they could get their hands on.

"You guys are going to have to catch up on the beers because Sabrina and I are ahead of you for sure."

"Oh, that sounds like a challenge," Matt said.

The whole table laughed and I was starting to feel like myself again. It was the first time in a long time that I was genuinely having a great time. We all enjoyed each others company.

"Dinner was great guys, thank you," I said. "Do we have room for dessert?"

The girls shook their heads, "No way, that was a lot of food." Hailey interjected.

"Yeah, I'm good too, I think I'm getting full on beer," Matt added.

"Okay fair enough. Let's get another round."

"Let's go swimming," Sabrina added. This was the greatest club. Offset from the private patio was our own pool with a Jacuzzi. There were different colored lights in the water to create a dancefloor effect. The design was impeccable and brought out the best vibe. We all got up, headed towards the pool, and slid down in. The water felt heavenly. A perfect mild temperature to feel refreshed and relaxed. Matt left to get us more beer and the partying really started to get serious.

As the night went on, everyone got pretty hammered. There were no awkward silences, it was just talking and laughing all night long. It was one of the best nights of my life. I could have easily had those girls around every night. The moonlight cast a reflection on the pool water as the party started winding down. Sabrina ended up passing out on the leather lounge chair looking quite sexy even in that state. Matt stood up ready to leave.

"I'm heading home you guys." He said with a slight slur.

"You can't drive home, you're too ," Nakita asserted.

"Oh, no worries little lady. I'll call an Uber."

"Why don't you just come and stay at my place, it's closer?" I said.

"I can't I have an early morning meeting and I can't risk sleeping in. It's just better if I'm home."

"Okay man, well, thanks for everything. Have a good night."

"Yeah, you too." I watched as Matt swayed out the door and I turned back to Nakita who was staring at me.

"I guess we should probably head home and get some sleep as well it's getting late."

I flashed her a charming smile then said, "Absolutely not. We are going to have some shots at my beach house. I'll get my driver to drive us."

"Shots?" She exclaimed. We were driven quick and stumbled into the house.

"Come with me." I grabbed her hand and led her towards the kitchen. I staggered when I got closer and Nakita snickered at me. We were like two crazy high school teenagers screwing around. The distance between us was small and I could feel the heat coming off of her. I felt my body respond to her close presence. Just looking at her turned me on, I could scoop her up and take her to my bedroom in a second, I didn't even care at that point about fucking things up.

"So, what kind of shots are we doing?" She asked with a sense of reluctance.

I took a deep breath trying to get those thoughts out of my mind. Looking around the room, I headed towards the liquor cabinet and pulled out a bottle of Jack Daniels and brought it back to the island that was in the center of the kitchen.

"Whiskey, oh god, you really are hardcore," she said with wide eyes.

I grinned. Grabbing a couple of shot glasses from the cupboard, I poured and handed her one and said, "Ready?"

"As ready as I'll ever be, I guess."

We raised our shot glasses and down the hatch they went. I took mine pretty well, but Nakita started coughing and laughing at the same time. "Oh man, that was brutal. I feel an awful burn. No more shots." She began to gag just a little. I was laughing, she looked cute as hell standing there sputtering after her shot.

"Sorry, maybe I should have picked something less harsh." Or maybe not, I was having such fun with her.

She wiped the burn induced tears from her eyes and stood there smiling. "No that's okay. I just don't normally drink whiskey. I forgot how strong it is."

Our eyes locked and we stared intently at each other. Suddenly, her smile faded a bit as we became entranced. My senses overwhelmed me and I forgot why I didn't care about fucking everything up. I could have cared less what those reasons were now.

CHAPTER EIGHT

NAKITA

The whole evening had been a blast and for the first time in a while I felt like I was living life to the fullest. I had been stressed out with auditions and with my career. I had thought of giving up and felt things were becoming hopeless, which wasn't like me. That night with the group, everything had been perfect and tons of fun. Sabrina and Matt had given up on the night a bit early and that left Eric and I with the chance to go back to the house and have more fun.

So, there I found myself, my throat still burning from the whiskey as I stared into his eyes. There was something happening that was inexplicable and I didn't know what to do about it. Eric reached down and kissed me; it happened in slow motion. That kiss wasn't like any I had ever experienced, it was hot and passionate. When our lips touched, a feeling of pure heat washed over my body. The energy between us was electrifying. When the tip of his tongue brushed mine, I found myself eager to suck on it. He was hot and sexy and I couldn't seem to get enough of his kisses. My heart raced and I became breathless the more he kissed me. Suddenly I shivered with the realization that his hand was seductively moving up my shirt caressing my stomach and then my breast. He unclasped my front closing bra with only a couple of fingers. I gasped as I continued to taste the sweetness of his kisses, which grew more passionate. My breasts were hardening and I was trying to catch my breath when we parted. We just stared at each other intensely, the heat between us was burning similar to a blazing fire.

"The whiskey on your lips Nakita is tantalizing."

I grinned, I loved the way he tasted as well, whiskey or not. My body was desiring so much more than what was being offered in that moment.

We kissed again. He pulled me into his arms and I could feel the heat coming off of his chest. This was nothing like the high school make out sessions I had had with my ex-boyfriends. He kissed me again and I inhaled his musky cologne, breathing through each kiss. His fingers were gliding through my hair making my scalp tingle and the hairs on the back of my neck rise. Every cell in my body was aching with anticipation of more.

He grabbed my hand and led me out of the kitchen. Our fingers entangled and every few steps he'd lean over and kiss my lips. As we approached the stairs, he kissed behind my ears and gently moved the tip of his tongue down my shoulder to my clavicle. I could feel the pulsing of my heart through my chest and the rushing of heat streaming down into the depths of my being. I wasn't thinking about what this would be like for the two of us and I didn't care. He would be my first and I wanted to feel every sensation. Was it stupid to lose my virginity to a man that I wasn't sure I would end up with? I wasn't and it didn't matter. All of this clouded my mind and right then I just knew that I desired him more than ever. I couldn't have said no to Eric even if I'd wanted to. My body yearned for him, I was eager for his touch.

He led me to his bedroom where he lifted me up and tossed me on the bed. I felt his bulging biceps harden as I grasped his arms out of surprise. I looked into his eyes and saw the passion consuming him. Without hesitation, I opened my legs and was ready to feel his strength against me. My libido was screaming for gratification. I wasn't sure what he had in mind, but I was up for anything. I kissed him hard, indicating my willingness to give myself over to him. My mind was racing as I watched him pull off his shirt and unzip his pants. I couldn't believe what was happening between us and yet it all felt so natural. We were both intoxicated, but neither of us cared about that, we were in the moment and ready to satisfy each others needs.

As he dropped his pants and black silk boxers my thoughts ceased. I gasped at his forwardness. I scanned every inch of his incredibly toned muscular body. God, he was hot. When our eyes met, he smiled, staring deeply and I know my face reddened when I smiled back. I took off my shirt and bra without any reluctance. I was ready and wanting. He leaned over, then dipped his head to lick the tips of my nipples. My body naturally let out a moan of satisfaction. His strong hands grabbed the sides of my miniskirt and curled his fingers around the edges of my panties pulling both down all at once. The magnitude of this first experience was extraordinary.

I had waited for this for so long that I didn't fear the dimensions of his body. His pecs were vibrating as he pulled my body closer to him and every vein was pulsating where it mattered most. His length and weight created a resonate feeling between my thighs. He was ready to take me and my body begged for him. I knew there would be pain, but the thought of the immense pleasure overrode any uncertainty.

"God, you are so beautiful. You're a sexy and striking girl Nakita."

He came over me, kissed my lips, and guided his hand between my thighs. With two fingers, he caressed me and every nerve ending fired in my body. I shivered and I felt myself tilt my pelvis in a more accepting position. I ached for more as he inserted his fingers... in and out. His respiration was heavier and I could see his body craving the need to be inside me. Seeing him throbbing sent satisfying chills throughout me.

"I love the way you feel, Nakita," I moaned as he increased the speed and rhythm of his fingers. My eyes fluttered. God, that felt so good. What was happening was unbelievable. My thoughts were incoherent while he was touching me. Was I really going to let him do this to me? I wondered if I should tell him I was a virgin, but he might stop and I couldn't have that. I was going to let him do everything and anything. I wanted it and needed it. I didn't care about anything else. I was hopeful this would be a good experience. Who was I kidding? Of course, it would be. Look at the man; he was built like The Rock and was made to make women scream his name. "Oooh, that feels so good Eric," was all I could say.

He smiled with a devilish charm and I put my hands behind his head pulling him into a passionate kiss. I had to suck on his tongue and I wanted to feel the fierce heat from his chest against mine. He moaned when I swirled the tip of my tongue around his. His loins quivered and I could feel him throbbing. I loved pleasing him and I wanted to do more of it. I wanted to taste every inch of him. He continued to kiss me as he used his fingers in ways I had never felt before. I was bombarded with waves of pleasure as though fireworks were being set off inside me.

As he removed his fingers, he caressed my backside and squeezed my ass. I flipped him over, surprising him. He didn't know my physical strength. I loved feeling his hands on me, they were amazing. I couldn't believe how turned on I was by his touch. I kissed his jawline and then nibbled on his lower lip. He growled and I bit down even harder. I slid my hands down his chest and between his hardened thighs. Using a firm, but steady pace I massaged upwards and downwards feeling every ripple.

The pulsation coursing through him was obvious on his face. I had never gone down on a man, but with him I was ready. I lowered my head and I licked the tip then circled the tiny hole. He expressed a low almost inaudible moan and then a slight shudder. I knew he was enjoying himself.

I took my fingernail tips and gently caressed his package while stroking him with my tongue. He let out a long moan as his fingers got lost in my hair. He tasted overwhelmingly salty like ocean water. I sucked hard and I loved the power that I had over him in my mouth. I was controlling every minute of the pleasure he was experiencing and I cherished it. He called out my name when I went full-throttle on him. Hearing him say 'Nakita' brought about immense excitement. It was more of a growl and my body created a deep need for him to be inside. I knew I needed him to be even more aroused before I let him enter my sweet spot.

"God, Nakita that feels ... incredible. Wow ... so good." He said breathlessly.

I continued to suck and twirl my tongue around his tip and lick up and down his shaft. His cock was hard in my mouth and taking it in brought me so much pleasure. I could feel myself getting wetter the more he throbbed against my tongue.

"Darling, I need to be inside you. Nakita, I'm going to fuck you so good. I can't wait to be deep inside of you."

As I slid him out of my mouth we switched positions on the bed. There was a fire in his eyes and I knew I was in for a night to remember. I lay back down on the bed, spreading my legs for him, and I caressed his chest with my feet, which drove him insane. He looked at my pussy as if he was falling in love with it and he climbed on top of me. He took his two long muscular fingers and massaged me fast enjoying the look of ecstasy that came over my face.

"Oh god...Eric come inside me, please. I want you so badly." I marveled at the fact that I was doing something I would never have considered before, but things with Eric seemed normal, that it shouldn't be any other way. I was more than happy to be screwed by him, in fact, I was aching to have him deep inside of me. I couldn't wait any longer.

I placed my feet on his hips and pulled him towards me giving him full permission to thrust passionately. I gasped as the full length of him that went inside, filling and expanding me. The burning pain was immediate, but the waves of pleasure came instantly, as well. I called out his name and he reacted by pumping in and out with more ferocity. Wow, everything about him confirmed all the rumors. He knew how to satisfy in more ways than one. He was everything I could ask for in a man.

"You feel amazing Nakita, I can't get enough of you. I love that you're so tight and I feel that I'm completely filling you."

My mind was barely functioning as the pure energy of sexual bliss was felt throughout my body. I had lost all ability to think and reason. I only saw him, felt him, and I had never felt so complete. A tension was building up inside of me and the intensity was unimaginable. He moved with intention and then gained momentum. Pumping repeatedly until I felt the build up heighten. I couldn't believe how good he felt inside of me.

Suddenly my muscles tightened around his throbbing cock and ecstasy came so strong it rocked my body and his.

He moved inside me slowly and then gained some momentum. He pumped inside of me repeatedly until I felt another build up happening. I couldn't believe how good he felt inside of me. It had been so long since I had sex that I forgot how wonderful it was to feel so close to someone. I couldn't have asked for a better lover. He felt incredible all around me and I felt faint as he pushed into me again and again.

"Oh Eric," I moaned. I could take his cock every single day, he felt amazing.

I felt the buildup increasing again and I moaned as another orgasm took me over. I couldn't get enough of him. He moved inside of me harder and I called out his name. "Oh Eric ... wow ... that feels so good."

He was looking down at me and he had a smile on his face. "God, you look hot when you orgasm."

I smiled, never imagining it would feel so good. The idea that there would be consequences to that moment didn't cross my mind. I needed him more than anything. I needed to feel fulfilled and he was the right man for sure.

"Oh Nakita, I'm going to cum."

I groaned as he said those words. He came soon after, expelling a loud moan. He fell breathless onto my chest and laid his head in the crease of my neck. I kissed his forehead and gently put my fingers through his hair. I felt so satisfied, I could have fallen asleep right then and there.

"That was amazing." He murmured.

I smiled, "I'd say. Drinks and then out of this world sex, thank you very much, Eric. Talk about a night to remember."

He chuckled. "I'm glad you enjoyed it."

I lay there feeling dizzy from the booze and the mind-blowing sex. He had felt so amazing between my legs it was more than I could have asked for. He got up to use the bathroom and I rolled over in bed, resting my head on his musky cologne smelling pillow. My whole body was warm from him and I had a smile on my face. I had never felt that good. Thinking of his hard body riding me was the last thought that came into my mind before passing out.

CHAPTER NINE
ERIC

Nakita and I never talked about our night of passion, it was like it never happened. I worried that she would be upset, but she just acted in character as if we were two people working together. Things between us were definitely different though, we had been getting closer than ever and I was enjoying my time with her. Things were coming to a close soon and I wondered what it would be like once she was gone.

We were out with Sabrina and Matt again and we left them to take a walk on the beach. The night was warm and the beach wasn't too crowded, so it was the perfect time for a stroll.

I wanted to spend some quality time alone with Nakita and a walk on the beach sounded like a perfect way to do that. My life had been so hectic lately that I couldn't even remember the last time I had taken a leisurely walk on the beach. Before Nakita came, the club scene was my focus, so visiting the many beaches of Miami rarely occurred to me. The sun was setting so the view was beautiful. The pink, purple, and orange hues blanketed the horizon. It was captivating. We both took off our sandals and let our toes sink into the soft sand that was starting to cool from the hot day. The sand between my toes felt nice. I would probably fall asleep as soon as my head hit the pillow that night. We walked in silence for a little bit, listening to the sounds of the waves and enjoying each others company.

As we continued walking I said, "Nakita, I just want to tell you how much I appreciate you being here."

She looked up at me with surprise and a slow smile forming on her face. I couldn't read her thoughts, her expressions were still perplexing since I hadn't known her long.

"What are you talking about?" she said.

"I know, I know. It's your job, but you've done such an amazing job already and the sponsors are thrilled with everything. The fact is you didn't just come down here and do the bare minimum to get the job done, which you could have, you genuinely helped me out. It's been fun having you around and that's why I'm thankful because it could have been a nightmare if we didn't get along."

She laughed, "I agree. But you don't have to thank me. I like being here and it wasn't at all what I expected either. I was worried that it would be weird or uncomfortable, but it hasn't been, not for a while anyway. It's fun here and you have helped me out as well and for that, I'm grateful for this opportunity. Things are good for me too, you know. I'm making money and doors are opening for me. We are helping each other."

"Good, I'm glad to have helped you out too. I want you to be happy. I think you are really going to go far in life. You're smart and you know what you want. Plus, you are beautiful, which is always a bonus in Hollywood."

She smiled slightly as her eyes drifted to the ground and I could see a blush forming on her cheeks. I don't think she realized just how beautiful she was or the kind of effect she had on me. This stunning girl was truly one of a kind.

We both got lost in thought. I thought back to the night we shared together and how much I wished we could do it again.

She was so sexy that night and free with herself. She wasn't inhibited at all like so many girls, she wanted to receive pleasure just as much as she wanted to give it. Thinking about sex was pretty easy with someone like Nakita, I genuinely liked her. She was great and there was so much to like about her. I was insanely attracted to her, which made it hard not to act on it sometimes. It would be nice to spend the night together without alcohol knowing there was a mutual wanting without any excuses getting in the way. I wasn't sure how possible that would be. She had been firm on the fact that we should just stick to business. I wanted to be close to her that night so badly, but I didn't know how to go about doing it without scaring her off. Nor did I want to do anything that would screw up our working relationship. She had already been so good to me so far, I didn't need my hormones wrecking anything.

"It's two weeks away before the Masters happen in Augusta. I can't believe how quickly time has passed." It was scary how close it was coming, but I was determined to focus properly this time and bring home the win.

She smiled, "I know. I'm really proud of you and I know you will get through things just fine. You are stronger than you think. I'm glad that doctor is helping you to focus on the good things in your life."

We exchanged a smile while when I said. "Thanks, Nakita. That's cool of you to say."

"You're welcome."

"You will be by my side, of course, helping to make everyone believe that our love affair is headed for marriage."

She laughed nervously, it was the most awkward laugh I'd ever heard. I laughed along with her not knowing what to say. Maybe I shouldn't have mentioned marriage. Would that be too soon? I hadn't dated a girl in so many years that I really didn't know what expectations there were these days. Lately, I had just been swiping left or right, without a care in the world.

We had to make people believe that we were marriage-bound, which was out of my comfort zone. People needed to believe that there was more going on between us than just casual dating. We would be okay though, Nakita had done an excellent job so far, and I wasn't worried about her ability to convince people of anything. She was one hell of an actress and if I needed people to believe that we were headed towards marriage, then she would make it happen.

I stopped walking and turned towards her. She stopped as well, looking up at me expectantly. Did she expect me to kiss her? I couldn't judge her expression at all.

"I thought you could come back and we could watch a movie. Maybe snuggle up and have some popcorn, keep each other warm for the night."

I hated myself for wanting to break parts of our contract, but I longed for her touch. I wanted to be close to Nakita, even if it was just snuggling in front of a movie. She was an amazing girl and if there was no job, I would have made her mine in an instant. We would be fucking like rabbits every single night. I wanted her by my side always and I had tried to keep my cool. I didn't make her uncomfortable enough to leave since our steamy night together, but at that point, I was sure she would stay the course, because we were friends now. I didn't want to push my luck, but if she agreed to watch a movie with me, then I would at least be happy with that.

She looked up at me and smiled, "Sure, I'm all for it," she said with a chuckle.

CHAPTER TEN

NAKITA

I opened the fridge in the kitchen to get a drink. We had been watching a movie for most of the night, which had really been a good idea. I loved snuggling up against him though I had a hard time concentrating the whole time. I couldn't even recall the name of movie, my heart beat hard the entire time, it was exhausting. I finally needed to get up to catch my breath and grab a glass of water. I brought the water jug to the counter and retrieved a glass from the cupboard. I was pouring when Eric came up behind me and wrapped his arms tightly around me. My eyes closed as I reveled in his embrace. I felt so safe in his arms and given his reputation I really shouldn't feel safe with him at all. He hugged me tightly, which made me feel completely amazing. He bent down and kissed my shoulder and chills radiated down my spine. My eyes fluttered closed and I remembered what it was like when he touched me.

"You are such a vixen, Nakita," he whispered against my skin and I felt the coolness of his breath, which left goosebumps.

"Oh, am I?" I said in a nonchalant manner.

"Yes, you have me falling for you, which is very dangerous."

I couldn't believe what I was hearing. He was falling for me?

I wondered if he was only playing, in the same way he played with so many other women in his life. Falling for Eric would be dangerous indeed, he was right about that. I was a good girl and he was a bad boy. Situations like these never ended well for the girl. When hadn't a bad boy broken a good girl's heart? I'm not sure there was ever an instance when it ever worked out. There I was with Eric tight against me whispering sweet nothings in my ear and I was falling right along with him.

"Are you just playing with me Eric, because I didn't think it was possible for the bachelor of the year to fall for anyone," I said jokingly hoping to lighten the mood. There were sparks flying and I didn't know how to get a handle on it.

He laughed, "Stranger things have happened."

I turned around and he released his grip on me, not that it mattered, because his mouth instantly seared me and I did nothing to stop it.

"I need you badly Nakita, my God it has been so long and I need to be inside you right now."

I couldn't catch my breath. I was completely speechless. What a turn-on to have a man talk to you that way; to show you he needed you that much. My body was warm all over at the thought of him taking me right there.

I kissed him, my tongue slid gently into his mouth, touching the tip of his tongue. Electricity flowed between us and the heat was emanating. Oh, God, what was with this guy? He had a way of taking over all of my senses. I felt mesmerized by him.

I smiled up at him, watching intensely. "I would like you to touch me." I said with a bit of desperation and desire.

He groaned. "Baby, that's all I want to do."

He grabbed my hand and led us to the bedroom. Tonight, we'd make passionate love. There were emotions in his eyes I hadn't seen before and I felt drawn to him in such a surprising way. Could we have a future together?

CHAPTER ELEVEN
ERIC

Friday arrived and so had the Masters. The crowds were thick and there was plenty of tension in the air. Everyone knew what was at stake and you could feel the fear and the nervous energy all around. I knew exactly what that feeling was like. I had been there multiple times and the feeling was always the same. I had reminded myself to focus and not think of what had happened in the previous years. The past didn't have to determine the present. I had a choice. I wasn't going to choke, not this time, not today. I needed this win.

I saw Matt talking with my sponsor and I walked over to them. They were chatting casually and they both seemed to be in good spirits.

"Hey, Eric how are you feeling today," asked Aria.

"As good as I can ... I suppose." I smiled, but I didn't feel like smiling at all. My emotions were starting to get the best of me. As I looked around, I saw my parents standing and talking to some of my peers. It would have been better if my father had stayed home. The last thing I needed to worry about was him breathing down my neck or possibly being disappointed in my performance.

Matt leaned over to me. "Relax man, it's going to be okay." Matt could see the tension in my face. I know I was clenching my jaw out of anxiety.

I nodded, appreciating the fact that Matt could read me like a book. I started to take more steady breaths in the hopes that my heart rate would slow down and I would feel less anxious. I couldn't believe how many people were here, it seemed like so many more than in past years. Though it was probably just an illusion of my mind. Things were beyond stressful for me at this point. I needed to listen to Matt's advice and chill out. It was only the beginning and we had a long way to go.

I left Matt and Aria to talk while I started to walk around. Matt called out to me that things would get started soon and not to wander too far. I waved him off and kept on going. I wanted to try to find Nakita and I wasn't sure where she would be. I had left the hotel earlier and I knew we'd meet up at some point. It wasn't long before I found her. I was completely caught off guard when I saw her. She was wearing a light pink sundress and her beautiful brown hair caught the sunlight reflecting light brown streaks. She was talking to a few random people and her smile was radiant. She couldn't have looked more beautiful even if she had tried. It was hard to picture life before Nakita came on the scene. She had become a staple in my life and I knew it was going to be very weird when she was no longer by my side. In fact, imagining life without her suddenly brought about a tightening feeling in my chest. Could I really go back to clubbing and taking random women home? I wasn't entirely sure that I could, it would seem so foreign after being with Nakita for three months. I had to wonder if I would think about Nakita the next time that I slept with another woman. We had been sleeping together for a while now and thinking of anyone else in my bed made my stomach queasy.

I approached her and pulled her away apologizing to the

people she was talking to. "Sorry, I need to steal this beauty for a moment," he said and Nakita laughed as she waved goodbye to them. She was glowing and I couldn't stop looking at her.

"Hey, handsome, how are you feeling today?"

"Not good to be honest with you."

"It's happening already? You need to think good thoughts."

"Well, maybe you should think about last night. Because it's been giving me good thoughts all day, that's for sure."

I laughed, "No kidding, it was great. You really do know how to make me feel good, don't you?"

"Well, I try." She said blushing.

I grasped her hand in mine and I looked around the event. There was a buzz in the air, but as long as I was with Nakita, I felt much better about things. I could do this, I was sure of it. I was determined to win this year. I just needed to focus and keep my eye on the prize. I looked at Nakita when I thought that. I didn't want her to go and that was certainly a new feeling for me. I wasn't in love with Nakita, but fuck if I didn't like her in my life more than I ever imagined! I felt so much that it made me sad that she was going to go away. I hated the thought of it, it drove me nuts just thinking about it. How long can I pay someone to play my girlfriend? I almost laughed, it was a ludicrous thought there was no way that Nakita would be okay with that. She wanted a life, a real life, she didn't want a pretend boyfriend for the rest of her life. She had a bright future and she deserved someone amazing to share it with.

I looked over at her and smiled. I leaned over and pulled her towards me, planting a big kiss on her sweet lips. I lingered with that kiss as long as I could, not wanting to let her go.

I heard a long awwww around us as we kissed and she started to laugh as we pulled apart. I smiled knowing that she thought we were just acting once again. The crowd really ate it all up and that probably wouldn't change.

"Well, I should probably get out there, the show is about to start."

She nodded, "Good luck, Eric. I'll be watching you. Just relax and you'll be fine."

I nodded and walked away from Nakita. I needed to find Matt so that we could get on the green and get the party started.

We were at the Augusta National Golf Club where the Masters were held every year. It was an exciting event and I was glad to be there. Matt and I walked to the first hole and waited our turn. If you won the Masters you received the Green jacket, it was the most prestigious reward for golfers all over the world and we were all vying for it.

Looking out on the fairway, I noticed the beautiful lush long ruff and the thickness of the green. The grass was much longer and thicker on either side of the fairway to challenge golfers. I started to think about the notoriously difficult twelfth hole. It was famous at Augusta and just the thought of it gave me cold sweats. It was only 150 yards, which was quite difficult even for the most seasoned golfer. I wasn't even close to that hole yet. I needed to pay all my attention to every hole leading up to it. The better I did the less I'd lose if I struggled at that hole.

Matt was carrying my bag. At the Masters, there were no carts, the caddies were there to carry bags, make suggestions, and ensure success. I turned to Matt who was smiling. It was my turn to go up and he gave me a thumbs up. He handed me the correct club as I approached the green and got into position. I knew every swing must be calculated with absolute precision.

I knew all eyes were on me and I decided to think of Nakita. She was out there somewhere watching me and probably casually talking to all the new people around her. She was proud of me already and that thought gave me a boost of confidence. I swung back, hit the ball with a whack, and saw it heading right for the hole. Unbelievable, I just hit a hole-in-one. I kept my cool, but I wanted to jump up and down with excitement. The crowd went wild and I was smiling ear-to-ear. Though caddies were supposed to stay calm, Matt was cheering loudly. I walked back over to him, whispered, "we got this", and handed him the club.

"One down, only seventeen more to go," he said with a laugh.

CHAPTER TWELVE

NAKITA

Walking to every hole was exhausting, but the thrill of seeing Eric lead over the other pros made it all worth it . I didn't realize the suspense that hole twelve would cause the golfers and the crowd. We stood holding our breath waiting to see who'd come out on top. I was a little worried at first. Eric chipped into the ruff, but others did it more than he. He ended up with a bogey, which was awesome since everyone else got double bogeys. It was crazy. In the end, he was 1-under par giving him the lead.

I screamed in excitement when I saw Eric make his shot and win the Masters. I was jumping up and down probably looking ridiculous, but I didn't care. He had won and I was insanely proud of him for doing so. He had finally made it, and I could see the pride washing over his face. He had his hand raised in the air, the club shooting for the stars, he looked so happy and tears filled my eyes as I watched him revel in his well-deserved win. Many people went up and congratulated him on the win. He deserved it and I was thankful that his parents were there to see it. His father would not be able to hound him any longer.

It was time for the customary passing off of the Green Jacket.

It was a Masters tradition with tons of pomp and ceremonial prestige. Last year's winner would put the Green Jacket on the new winner. Perry Davenport approached Eric and presented him with the jacket and shook his hand. Eric was elated even a bit tearful. I stood off stage beaming with such pride for him.

Eric's parents were there suddenly surrounding him with congratulations and hugs. His father was practically glowing. I was happy for the whole family. His father looked very proud of his son and I hoped that that pride would last a long time. Eric deserved to be there with all the hard work he had put into this. He had finally made it. I was happy that he no longer had to be the laughing stock in front of the media. I decided to make my way over to him and congratulate him myself.

As soon as he saw me, he threw his arms around me, picking me up and spinning us.

"Congratulations, I'm so happy for you," I said feeling a bit dizzy and smiling fervently.

He planted a lovingly intense kiss on me. I melted into his arms, not caring that his parents were standing beside us. We parted and I looked over at them and almost laughed at the surprised expressions on their faces.

"Hi, I'm Nakita. It's nice to meet you."

"Nakita, it's a pleasure. You have changed our son, he's barely recognizable."

Eric rolled his eyes as I almost laughed out loud, "Oh I didn't do anything. He was always in there somewhere."

"Well, it's just wonderful having you here."

"Thank you, you must be very proud of Eric," I said looking at him and winking.

"Oh, we are," said his father.

"Very proud," his mother added. She was beaming at her son and it appeared as if they were both genuinely happy for their son.

Eric turned to me and kissed me on the forehead. I loved when he did that, I felt so cherished.

"Thank you Nakita for all your help. Most especially for believing in me."

I smiled, "Of course, I believe in you. I always have and I always will. You're an amazing golfer, you just needed to believe in that yourself."

"I know. But I couldn't have done it without your help."

I started laughing, "Me too, you bad boy."

He kissed me again on the lips and then I pulled away from him as other people started coming up and congratulating him.

I watched as he got dragged off into the crowd. I had never seen him happier than this and he deserved every bit of the attention. Tears begun to build in my eyes as I knew things were coming to a close. It was finally over and although I was happy for him, I was also very sad that it had to end so quickly. Suddenly an arm wrapped around my shoulder and I looked over in surprise to find Matt there smiling.

"Hi, Matt! You scared me."

He laughed, "Oops, sorry. Are you all caught up in the moment?"

"Yeah, what a great moment."

"I'd say. I'm proud as hell of him. What a game he played today. I got worried a couple of times, but he pulled through. Fuck, he really deserves this win, it's been a long time coming."

"Yeah, he looks so happy, doesn't he?"

"Yes, he does. So, are you ready for a big ass celebration or what?"

"Hell yeah, I am."

He grabbed my hand and led me away. We would leave and go back to the hotel where they had arranged to have a huge party in one of the banquet halls. His parents had spared no expense. This was a great way for me to forget my job was ending soon or rather the relationship that felt so real.

The party was insane and there were so many people. I often got lost in the crowd, it was overwhelming. I was pretty much on my own except for the times I would find Matt in the crowd. Eric was busy, surrounded by all his fans, as well as his friends and family. Everyone was basking in his glow and wanted a piece of him now that he was a big winner. I didn't want to intrude on his night, so I decided to go up to the hotel room and relax. I needed to separate myself from him anyways. The job was over and I would be returning home soon. There was no point in me being attached to his hip when the job was technically over.

When I got back to the room, I laid out on the bed and thought about the long day. I was proud of the job that I did, getting Eric to where he needed to be in order to win. I sat up and pulled my purse over to me. I pulled the contract out of my purse and read it over slowly. I was literally flying out the next morning and returning home. Just like that, it was all over. The gig was up and my job was done. Eric did what he needed to do and now the whole world loved him. I could totally understand that feeling.

Just then there was a knock on the door. Confused I went to answer it and there stood Eric on the other side.

"Hey, what are you doing? Why aren't you at your party?"

"Well, I noticed you left and I missed you."

I laughed, "Eric you should be down there enjoying your victory. You deserve it."

"It's not as much fun without you."

I frowned as I moved back into the hotel room. He followed me and closed the door behind him. "What's wrong?"

"Eric, I leave tomorrow. I have an audition for a movie. It looks like all the publicity paid off."

He swallowed hard. "I know. But, what if you didn't leave?"

"Eric, what are you talking about?"

He came close and caressed my cheek before tipping my chin upwards, "So much has changed over the past few months. I know this was a job for the both of us, but I don't feel that way anymore. I don't think you do either," he said with such seriousness.

"Eric, explain yourself. I thought you wanted to get back to your old life."

"Screw that, I don't. I'm falling for you Nakita and I don't want you to go. Stay here with me and let's see if we can give this a real shot. You can still go to your audition. You can live here instead and let's see where this goes."

I was shocked. I couldn't believe what I was hearing. He wanted me to stay? Eric Vanlare wanted me to be his real girlfriend, it was all so unbelievable. We had been acting all this time, well sort of...there had been some really great slip-ups. But at the end of the day, I'd thought I would just go home and return to my old life. Now he was proposing that I stay and try out a real relationship with him. I wasn't sure what to think. I wanted it, with him, I did, but could we just transition like that? No longer act and really to be together, I wasn't sure.

"I don't know Eric. This is all so strange."

He laughed, "I know it is. I wish I would have met you in a normal way. But here we are and I'm asking you to stay with me. I'll help you get your own place. Work on your career from here and just let's see where it goes. Please Nakita, don't walk away from me."

Well, how could I say no to something like that. I smiled at him. "Okay, you win. I won't leave. Let's do this craziness and see where it leads us."

He seemed ecstatic and pulled me in for a kiss. When our lips met, that same familiar heat flowed through us. He was falling for me, but I was already there. I had met the man of my dreams in the most bizarre situation ever, but we would have one hell of a story to tell our grandchildren.

We pulled apart and stared at each other.

"To the future," I said.

He kissed me on the forehead. "To the future."

The End

SIGN UP TO RECEIVE FREE BOOKS

Sign Up to Receive Free E-Books and Audiobook Codes.

Would you like to read **The Unexpected Nanny, Dirty Little Virgin** and **other romance books** for **free?**

You can sign up to receive these free e-books and audiobooks by typing this link into your browser:

https://www.steamyromance.info/free-books-and-audiobooks-hot-and-steamy/

Or this one:

https://www.steamyromance.info/the-unexpected-nanny-free/

PREVIEW OF THE VIRGIN'S BARGAIN

A Billionaire Romance Story

By Eliza Duke

Blurb

Catherine:

There are two men in my life right now; one of them I don't want to live without, and the other, I may die from. Morty Branch has been cyberstalking me for unknown reasons for six months and just announced that he knows where I live and is coming for me. I need help—fast. And the only man I have to turn to is the man of my dreams. But who is Sergei? How is he so confident that he can take care of my stalker problem? And how do I compensate him? I don't have anything to offer him that he wants besides my virginity—or so I think. When he comes up with a counter offer, it intrigues me. He'll protect me ...and in return, I'll be his for one week.

Sergei:

I just had a sweet, little virgin offer me her body in return for protection. Were I a lesser man, I would have taken her up on it. But I don't take advantage of desperate women—and this one is very desperate indeed. Instead, I lay down a simple rule: I will protect her in return for her living as my own for one lovely week. Her agreement is bound to make things interesting for me as I solve the mystery of her persistent, now murderous stalker. But when my own dark side of life frightens my Catherine away, I must find and save her before Morty Branch makes his move.

CATHERINE

I'm daydreaming about my neighbor, Sergei, when I check my email and the ten new messages shock me back to reality. All are from the same sender, all have attachments, and none of them do I want to open under any circumstances. The flesh-colored thumbnails at the bottom of my screen tell me enough.

The tall, dashing Slavic hunk who lives in the building penthouse vanishes from my mind for the first time in hours as I stand up from my desk chair. I can't deal with this right now. I leave the walk-in closet that serves as my computer nook and hurry into the kitchen to make myself a cup of tea.

I start crying a little as the tea brews in my tiny, purple, clay teapot. The tears have lots of fuel: confusion, grief, embarrassment, fear, shame, and even anger at both myself and the author of the emails. It takes a few minutes before I can force myself to stop.

Somebody help me, I scream inside my head. I've changed my email address five times in six months and changed my phone number four times. The authorities know; I send them everything he sends to me, but they have never done anything useful for me.

Morty, my stalker, started out as a friend I made online. I don't go out much at all, thanks to my health, and so I have almost no friends offline. I thought he was twenty and from my hometown back in Seattle. He told me that he was a fuel engineer at a plant my father used to own. He claimed that he got curious about me when I managed to make the papers a few times with my art.

Morty was polite and intelligent, completely unlike all those nauseating creeps I always end up blocking. He responded in ways that made it clear he was actually reading what I wrote and cared about my point of view. He made me feel safe, and so eventually, we got to exchanging —pictures—just normal ones, no nudes.

I'm shy about cameras. There's nothing particularly bad about my appearance, except of course for how young and vulnerable I look. I'm five-foot-nothing and slim, with wavy chestnut hair, pale skin, and big, light-brown eyes.

His photos show a guy a little older than me, who is a little weak-chinned and chubby, but kind-faced, with big, brown eyes and spiky, brown hair. He apparently liked nineties-era vintage clothes, including loose, light, stonewash jeans and trench coats. Not gorgeous, but I didn't care, especially at the time.

Not everyone can be the mysterious, wealthy man upstairs, whom I wish I could go back to daydreaming about again. I could have walked around in a happy haze this evening and gone to bed hugging my pillow and wondering what Sergei's thick, black hair smells like. Instead, here I am dealing with Morty's shit.

Again.

We spent almost a month corresponding online before he did anything ... off. But when he removed his cloak of civility, what a monster was revealed beneath. I don't know what exactly set him off after the end of that first month. I wasn't dating anyone else, so it wasn't jealousy. I didn't have an argument with him, do anything that he could possibly find insulting, or blow him off. But one day, out of the blue, he emailed me calling me a rich, crazy whore and told me that he wanted to fuck me with a knife.

I didn't believe it was Morty at first. It was such a complete change from the personality he had shown before that I was sure that someone had hacked his account! But no such luck. As soon as I wrote him on his Facebook to confirm, he repeated his horrifying threat, along with several more.

I was so shocked that I reported him at once, blocked his email address, and contacted the police. After furnishing copies of the threats to the cops, along with Morty's photos, I hoped that was the end of it. But, of course, it wasn't.

Morty has now been sending me threatening emails from different throwaway addresses for the last six months. Most of them are sexual, full of rape-porn images, and descriptive about what this raging creep wants to do to me as soon as he gets his hands on me. But, lately, it's getting to be a lot less porn and a lot more torture.

It's not just a matter of some guy being such a pissy fuckboy that I don't want to date him. This asshole is terrorizing me, and thanks to the things I foolishly confided—what can I say? I was lonely— he knows exactly how much his harassment is affecting me.

I've had PTSD with agoraphobia and panic attacks since my family died in an explosion when I was five. I don't like going outside, and I have trouble staying in rooms with more than four other people. Loud noises, especially fireworks, gunshots, or movie explosions can terrify me into a panic attack or worse—a flashback.

I take medication, meditate, exercise, see a therapist, and force myself to leave my home regularly. I'm still pretty much a shut-in, though. I'm not proud of this fact; I didn't even admit it to Morty until last month.

Fortunately, I received a big insurance settlement along with my inheritance from my parents. This lets me support myself, despite my problems. The apartment is big, secure, and luxurious, I have my own glassed-in balcony that I use as a greenhouse, and I even have a spare bedroom I was able to convert into a small art studio.

My life isn't too bad most of the time, although my friends are minimal, and the closest I have ever come to love is preoccupying myself with my mysterious neighbor. But in the age of the Internet, I can order almost everything I need online, from sushi to a ride to my therapist.

I take a deep, steadying breath and try to collect my thoughts. The chamomile tea is starting to fill the air with its sweet, delicate scent. I grab my favorite kitten mug and pour the golden liquid into it, then add a dollop of raw honey and stir.

I sip and read news on my phone silently for a while. Inside, I'm shoring myself up with the usual reassurances. Each one wears away a little bit at my fear, until I can think again.

Morty is a coward. All he ever does is talk. There's no chance that he will actually try to make good on any of these sick "promises" of his. None at all.

I am almost to the point where I could consider looking at those damn emails. But I stay there anyway, breathing deep and slow while I cast around inside my head for something else to focus on.

There's Sergei, at least.

Sergei, who lives in the penthouse, owns the building—among several others in the neighborhood. He is the kind of rich that even my father never aspired to, and no one has any idea how he came by it. There are so many rumors about our hot, aristocratic-looking landlord that I don't know where the truth lies.

Even so, thinking about him is like slipping into my jacuzzi: warm, relaxing, and leaving me tingling all over. It doesn't take all the fear and anger away, but it does rest my mind for a moment.

Is he a secret descendant of Russian aristocracy? Is he a criminal? Is he a reclusive artist? A novelist? A refugee from Putin's Russia made very, very good?

I have absolutely no way of knowing, and the mystery that shrouds Sergei makes him all the more attractive to me. Not that he needs any help in that department. He has all the intensity and athleticism of a military man and all the elegance of a man of breeding.

Tall and commanding, powerful in build, and meticulously well-dressed, he looks like the kind of man who lives in a castle, with a crown on his brow. Thick, wavy, jet-black hair spills around his strong, narrow face, with white skin, sensually curved lips, and narrow, deep-green eyes. His voice is deep and resonant, with a touch of a Russian accent.

I first ran into him when we shared an elevator on the way up from the lobby. I was coming from my afternoon therapy session, fragile-feeling and tired, and was relieved to have the mirror-walled elevator to myself. But before the doors closed, a tall figure in a black, wool overcoat stepped in through the gap.

I froze like a deer in my corner as he moved into the small space, his spicy cologne teasing my nostrils. He barely noticed me, busy with whatever conversation he was having on his cell phone. The conversation was in Russian, which I don't speak a word of, but the all-business tone to his voice was unmistakable.

I stared at the black curls that escaped from beneath his fur-trimmed hat as he rumbled authoritatively into his smart phone.

I glimpsed that narrow, intense face of his, but round, black sunglass lenses covered his eyes. I felt a strange, melting warmth, leaving my muscles loose but my heart pounding.

I wanted to ask who he was, but I didn't dare interrupt his phone call. I only found out later that this magnificent man was our landlord and the occupant of the building penthouse. By then, I already had a catastrophic crush on him.

I have never dared talk to him, not in an entire year of living here. I daydream about him when I take my walks, when I lie down for naps, or stretch out for the night's sleep. But aside from a curious glance now and again as I pass him in the lobby, Sergei Ostrov has never noticed me.

One day, maybe, I will get up the courage to talk to him in person. I have no idea what I'll say, but I want to try. Meanwhile, though, I'm forced to content myself with some very pleasant wishful thinking.

Daydreaming about Sergei does the trick; I'm smiling a little again by the time I finish my cup of tea. I get up to face the mess on my computer, bringing an extra mug of chamomile with me.

I let my eyes blur a little as I open each email in turn, avoiding the photographs. I don't know where this sicko, Morty, finds so many photographs of brutalized women, but I don't have to open them, and I never do. I send it all on to the cops and get it the hell out of my inbox.

Morty spends the first nine emails berating and threatening me in ways that are starting to become formulaic again.

Threats involving knives, kitchen implements, and sexual violation.

Demands that I answer.

Whiny pleas that I'm hurting his feelings by not answering.

All followed by more threats.

I hold my own through the nine-email tantrum and send them on without comment to my contact at NYPD. But then I open the last one, and the two lines of text send me into an instant panic.

The first line is my home address, along with the door code to my building. The second consists of four words:

I'm coming for you.

SERGEI

I'm standing in the corner of an underground meeting room, still and silent as a statue in one of my best dark, silk suits. My cousin, Mikhail, local boss for the Russian mob, sits casually at a desk at the front of the room. He smooths his white-blond hair back from his high forehead as he looks over the debtors that my men and I have brought to him. "Bring the first of them forward, Andrei."

Andrei, a brute with a blocky face and Russian prison tattoos, moves forward to lead the first of the serious debtors forward. It's Friday night: time to settle the weekly accounts. Each one owes us at least ten thousand dollars, and tonight they will either pay up or tell us how else they plan to compensate us.

There are seven of them, all races, all ages, all male, except for the underage-looking girl standing with one of the older men. My eyes rest on her for a moment; she's tiny, with innocent eyes and soft, undefined features. The man with her is skinny, twitchy, and very nervous. He's jonesing.

I wince, and Mikhail and I exchange glances before he turns to speak to the tiny, Arab man in the white, pillbox hat that Andrei brought forward.

A few of our "guests" have already noticed the plastic tarps lining the floor. An older man in a dull-brown suit keeps glancing down at them, tears clinging to the insides of his glasses. The girl stomps at a small wrinkle on one of the tarps and peers at it with a curious expression.

Someone has dressed her into a short, red, velvet dress that shows off her skinny shoulders and high-heeled shoes. The outfit's too old for her, as is the red lipstick she's wearing. This is a child, and from the way she is acting, she thinks this is all some kind of game.

One of my eyebrows twitches upward. The dozen of our men lounging against the walls start to notice my reaction and then what's causing it. They shuffle and mutter to each other in Russian, uncomfortable with the tiny girl's presence in a place where someone could easily get shot.

Even the hardest man in Russia has his limits. Kids are usually part of that. You don't mess with kids in our territory unless you are suicidal or completely stupid.

I'm not sure yet which one our debtor here is. But his forcing an oblivious little girl into this situation makes my blood boil. I'm no saint, but children and other such utter innocents are always off limits, no exceptions. One glance at Mikhail tells me that he's annoyed as well. Right now, though, we both have a job to do.

Mikhail calls each man forward in turn, working through the first three, extracting apologies, promises of payment, and in one case, a large bankroll. He tosses the latter to me and I riffle through it quickly: "Fifteen thousand even."

That guy, the weepy old man, goes free right away with a huge sigh of relief. The outer door of the warehouse we're in opens briefly, letting in a harsh beam of light, then creaks shut again after him.

The other adults seem relieved, understanding that my boss

is good as his word, and if they just pay up, that's the end of it. Of course, after today, things will get very complicated for those who try to drag their feet on paying. And the offers they make tonight will have to be pretty damn good.

When his time comes, the older man grabs the little girl by the upper arm and pulls her forward, a nervous smile on his lips. Mikhail stops leaning on the desk and unfolds his arms, peering at the man as he comes to a stop a few feet away.

"I don't have your money for you yet," the man stammers at Mikhail. "But I've brought you something to make up for it."

Before we can say anything, he puts his hands on the girl's shoulders and shoves her out in front of him. "Go," he orders her, and she looks back at him in confusion. "You are to go with these men, now!" he insists.

Mikhail and I look at each other again. I may not be entirely surprised, but that doesn't make me feel any less sick. Pushing out of my corner, I walk over to them.

The man's head snaps around, and his eyes widen as he sees me coming. I ignore him and crouch down in front of the little girl, looking into her soft, brown eyes. "Hello there," I say in English.

"Hi," she says, rocking a little and nibbling on one finger.

"How old are you?" I ask, keeping my tone as kind and calm as I can.

"She's fifteen—" the man tries to cut in. I snap my head around and fix him with a stare. Those who know me know that stare means danger. Those who don't know me typically think that stare means death. When it involves scum like this guy, that assumption is almost always right. Paling, he goes quiet. He glances around at the exits, as if assessing his chances of surviving a run for it.

"I'm eight," the girl pipes up, and the man looks at her in

horror. "Why did Uncle Willie say I was fifteen? Why do I have to go with you? Will my mommy be there?"

Barely marshalling my temper, I think of the girl's mother and the hell she's probably going through right now with her child missing. "I will take you back to your mommy as soon as this meeting is over," I promise. Again, I'm no saint, but I always keep my promises. It won't take me much effort to put her situation right.

Unfortunately, there's another part to the problem and he's losing all color in his face as I go quiet. The little one and her trash-fire of an uncle must be dealt with separately.

I turn my head to stare down the man, who is now looking between myself and the child with his mouth a perfect, mute 'O'. "You brought Mikhail an eight-year-old girl?"

"She's old enough," Willie stammered out after a moment. "I swear to God she's old enough. Just, please, take her! I don't got nothing else to pay my debt with!"

"So you kidnapped your niece, you dog?" I snap as I move back gently from the girl and stand up.

I can't stop glaring at this twisted, skinny little man with his meth teeth and his way of rubbing his face every few seconds. He's so grotesque, hunkered behind this child and begging that we take her ...for what? What kind of creatures does he think we are?

I know, though I hate it. He thinks that we are like him. No honor, no mercy, and no restraint of any kind.

"Please don't call Uncle Willie a dog," the girl says in her clear voice.

I look down, my eyebrow going up again, this time in amusement. "I'm sorry, what was that?"

"Please don't call Uncle Willie a dog," she pleads again. "That's mean to dogs. Dogs are nice."

I start to —laugh—but then hear Willie curse her under his breath. The bastard has only the smallest of ideas of how much trouble he's in. Immediately, I'm all business again. "Of course. Let me finish with your uncle, and I'll take you home."

I turn to Willie as I speak, and despite my kind tone in answering her, my eyes hold all my rage. His own eyes go round in absolute terror as the truth works its way through the meth, booze, and stupidity. He's fucked up worse than if he had just come here with turned-out pockets and a plea.

I gesture to one of our —men—Nicolai, a new father whose wife is a kindergarten teacher. "Nicolai, I've got a job for you," I call over in Russian.

Once Nicolai has gone to watch deliberately loud cartoons with Willie's niece a few rooms away, I turn to Willie, wearing my coldest expression. "You're living on your sister's couch, correct?"

Willie blinks in shock that I've done my homework. "Yeah," he mutters after a moment. "Why?"

"So, you conned your big-hearted sister into taking you in. Then, in return for her kindness, you menaced and then kidnapped her extremely underage daughter. Yes?" My accent gets thicker and my English worse the angrier I get, but Willie gets my meaning.

He gulped. "Wait, please, sir, just hear me out—"

"Hearing you out was exactly what Mikhail planned to do." I pull my Glock with its Glaser safety round loads from the holster beneath my leather blazer and hold it down at my side as he starts to shiver. "He still would, if you had not insulted his honor by implying that he would do anything to a child."

I point my pistol at his face and pull the trigger as he's drawing his breath to scream. The debtors who are still waiting to see Mikhail cringe as Willie's corpse falls to the floor, minus an eye. There is no exit wound. I feel no remorse. Yes, I am a killer. I kill street trash like Willie. And I will never regret it.

I look to Boris, another of my subordinates. "Get the cleaners up to take care of this before we bring the girl out," I order him as I go back to my corner. I know that rumors of this will get around, making sure that nobody ever tries to pay Mikhail in kidnapped children again.

It's almost midnight before I get the little girl, whose name is Amy, to walk up the street to the door of her Brooklyn brownstone and knock on it. She's none the worse for wear, with a tummy full of kid-sized cheeseburger and a strawberry shake. Her lack of interest in her uncle, given how sweet the little girl is, speaks volumes. She's not concerned about his wellbeing because, clearly, intuition told her he was a very bad man. Children know those things better than adults. They trust their instincts.

That's the last time that anyone ever saw—or will ever see--Willie. The cleaners are very thorough. Anyone we kill disappears, thanks to them.

I watch through my spyglasses from behind my black Lexus as she pushes the intercom button and speaks for a while. Less than a minute passes before a short, round woman with Amy's hair bursts out the door and scoops her up into a hug, sobbing.

The woman lets out an explosive sneeze before turning and sweeping her child inside. In my head, I can put her bit of the story together, or at least make an educated guess. Mom, drugged out on cold medicine, trusted her brother to at least look after her kid. Whatever Amy tells her won't matter in the end; Willie's gone and the kid is safe. Hopefully her mother will never be so trusting again.

Willie died too fast and with too little pain. Maybe it's best that the poor woman slept through the most of it. If the police had already been there when I showed up, returning Amy would have been a lot tougher.

I'm done for the night. I get back in my Lexus and head toward my favorite bar in Central Park West, walking distance from my penthouse. I want a stiff drink and a woman for the night. I'll settle for the drink.

CATHERINE

I've tried to sleep for hours, ever since crying myself into exhaustion, but I can't. *Morty knows where I live.*

I don't know how he found me. He doesn't seem that good with computers, and I know I haven't left my information anywhere online. I'm too careful.

But he has my address, and now I must do something about it. Otherwise my home will never feel safe again. The only problem is, I have no one reliable to help me.

The police certainly don't count. They don't have a suspect to arrest, no one to file a restraining order against, and they won't spare an officer to watch over the building. I hung up after they suggested that at my income bracket I should have a bodyguard anyway.

They had a point, but having a bodyguard would mean letting some stranger into my life full-time. Thanks to my issues, the idea of sharing my precious apartment with some total stranger horrifies me.

But then I start to think about the apartment building where I live. Morty will have to get into it to get at me. If I can't get those who are supposed to protect the city to help me, maybe I can get the building owner to do something.

Sergei. I sit up in bed at the very thought, clutching the covers to my breasts. I'm considering finally talking to him, but doing even more than that: begging for his mercy and his aid.

He's wealthier than I have ever been. He doesn't need my money. But I should have something that he wants.

I still have my father's Matisse and Picasso and my mother's wedding jewelry, but I don't know how attractive an offer they will make for him. There's something else that I have that I'd rather give him, but using it in commerce makes me uncomfortable. I'm still a virgin.

These days, it's not unheard of. With the Internet providing anonymity and the ability to connect with people all over the globe, it's actually gotten fairly easy. A lot of young women sell their virginities.

But am I that mercenary? I know I'm that desperate, but do I have the nerve to do it? Would I even be considering it if I wasn't already so besotted? The answer to that last question, at least, is very definitely no. I'm no martyr.

I get up and get dressed in a bulky, snuggly, blue sweater and jeans,

It's probably very stupid for me to be wandering out in the middle of the night, now that my stalker is in town and knows my address. But I can't stay: the plan I'm considering is too crazy and I need to walk.

There's a bar two blocks from the apartment building. I'm not much of a drinker; the sedatives kill my tolerance and make it dangerous for me to drink too much. But there's one thing about that dark, little bar with all the gilding and mirrors that draws me far more than booze: Sergei goes there a lot.

When returning home from my evening therapy sessions, I have spied him bellied up to the bar or sitting at a corner table many times. I always look for him whenever I walk by its big, gilt-decorated window. When I see him, I always linger, drinking in the sight of him for as long as I dare.

I've always wanted to go in and have a drink. Maybe sit at that corner table and imagine what it would be like to sit there with him, drinking and talking ...like a couple on a date.

I bundle up, covering my hair and swathing myself in a dark, gray, wool overcoat that gives me a mannish look. I want no one to know who I am, or even that I'm female.

My heart starts beating fast as I make my way out the front door. It's been raining lightly, leaving the sidewalks more deserted than usual. New York is the city that never sleeps, but that doesn't mean the people here like getting soaked.

I walk the two blocks, looking around often, wary of anyone following me. No one does, or if they do, they're better at stalking than I am at picking them out. I force myself to trust that the latter isn't true as I spy the bar storefront up ahead.

There's a knot of drunken men on the sidewalk outside the door. I'll have to pass them to go inside. One of them swivels his head and locks his gaze on me like a targeting system as I approach, and my stomach starts flipping over.

He's ugly in a brutal way, his hair greasy and his face like a fist, except where his grin splits it. His tiny eyes are just gleams in the deep pits beneath his brows and he stumbles forward, grabbing for me as I get in range.

I step aside immediately and duck into the bar. I hear him curse behind me as the other men laugh at him. *Please, let that be the end of this.*

I glance around, but can't see any sign of Sergei. My heart sinks and I hurry toward a clear spot at the bar, knowing it will be harder for this creep to do anything if he's in full view of a lot of people.

I don't get three steps before a meaty hand closes on my upper arm. "I'm talking to you, bitch!"

Oh, God. My mind goes blank with terror; I stiffen up like a manikin as he starts dragging me backward. *No, don't touch me, leave me alone, someone help—!*

No one seems to notice as he drags me, mute and stiff with terror, toward the door. I want to cry out for help, but my voice sticks in my throat. I try to catch the bartender's eye, but he stares right past me as he polishes glasses.

My mind is starting to go blank, a flashback boiling up from the depths of my skull and filling my vision with flying rubble and fire. He's going to take me somewhere and rape me. No one is going to help—

"Stop right there."

The deep, accented voice is so familiar and unexpected that, for a moment, I wonder if I am dreaming.

The man stops and snorts, turning around while dragging me with him. When he sees Sergei standing in the doorway behind him, he goes very, very still.

I look up and the fire recedes from my brain as if blown out by a blast of icy air. Sergei stands there in his deep, blue, wool coat, hair loose on his shoulders, removing his fur-trimmed hat with one hand. The other hangs at his side casually, with a dark, snub-nosed revolver in it.

"Let the young lady go," Sergei rumbles, staying very calm, but staring unblinkingly into the older, fatter man's eyes.

The man looks over at me, his grip loosening a little already, and then turns his head again to take in Sergei. He licks his lips with a thick, purplish tongue, then lets me go.

"Should keep her closer if she's yours. Stupid little slut." He gives me a shove toward Sergei, and an iron hand shoots out to steady me as a whiff of spicy aftershave washes past my nostrils.

"She is not mine—the bar is. You are banned, *cacat*. Get out and do not return." He gives an imperious flick of the revolver, barely raising it from his side.

The man's jaw drops. He glances down at the revolver, then slinks out, giving Sergei a wide berth. I'm left standing frozen, right in front of the man of my dreams, with his hand still on my shoulder.

My heart is still beating fast, but the fact that he rescued me is sinking in.

He pockets the pistol as casually as a man putting away his cell phone, and concern breaks across his stern features. "Are you all right?" he asks.

My mouth opens, but my throat is still closed. I can't speak—yet, and to my deep surprise, his face falls as he instantly seems to recognize this. "No, clearly you are not."

He calls something in Russian over to the blank-faced bartender, who nods and lumbers into the back. Sergei ushers me over to the corner table and gets me sat down in a chair. A few moments later, the bartender comes over and sets a pot of steeping tea and a pair of cups on a trivet in front of me.

Sergei settles into the other chair to watch as I start to move and look around. "Are you back?" he asks in a low, calm voice after about a minute.

Something clicks into place inside of me, and I nod. "I ...am. Thank you." My voice is weak, but the words finally come out.

"You live in my building." It's not a question. He leans forward toward me, brow furrowing slightly. Then he nods once. "Catherine White, the heiress."

He doesn't mention the story behind my inheritance, though everyone who makes the connection between that name and my face knows the story. My parents' deaths, along with those of four-hundred-and-fifty-three other people, had made international news. I'm really glad that Sergei doesn't bring it up.

"Yes. I ...I have seen you around, but I'm bad at starting conversations." My cheeks tingle with heat, and I see him break into a faint smile.

"I am Sergei Ostrov, your landlord." He tilts his head, curiosity gleaming in his hard, green eyes. "What brings you out on the streets this late? It is not your normal habit."

I blink at him, words sticking in my throat again. He noticed my comings and goings? He actually knew that I existed all this time?

He chuckles at my amazement. "I make it a point to keep an eye on things around my properties. I do not abide outsiders disturbing the peace of my tenants."

The idea of him watching every night over his tiny kingdom makes me feel safer. "You ...watch over the neighborhood?"

"Not alone. I have a security team that assists in monitoring the ten blocks that I own." Ten blocks in Central Park West. That makes him a billionaire all by itself.

How did he make the money to break into the most lucrative real estate market on the Eastern Seaboard? *Yet another mystery.* He fascinates me more by the minute.

He pours the tea: some mixture of herbs, brewed very strong. I can smell chamomile in there somewhere. He slides a cup over to me, and I take it, warming my fear-chilled hands on it. My eyes dart to his own hands, so large and, from a few minutes back when one rested on my shoulder, so warm.

He pours for himself. "Something upset you, I suspect, or you would not have left the haven of your home. Am I correct?"

I pause with my trembling cup halfway to my lips, then set it down. He watches me and waits, neither coaxing me nor changing the subject. Finally, I manage to nod.

I'm drained from fighting flashbacks= and still not quite sure how I should approach him. But there's no choice ...and if he has an interest in tenant security, he should know about the threat to it.

"I need your help, Mr. Ostrov."

If you want to continue reading this story, you can get your copy from your favorite vendor by searching for the title:

<u>The Virgin's Bargain</u>
<u>A Billionaire Romance Story</u>

You can also find the e-book version by typing this link in your computer's browser:

https://www.hotandsteamyromance.com/products/the-virgin-s-bargain-a-billionaire-romance

OTHER BOOKS BY THIS AUTHOR

Saving Her Rescuer: A Billionaire & A Virgin Romance

I WAS JUST TRYING to get away from my crazy ex for the weekend when I ended up in a giant pileup on the highway up to Gore Mountain.

HTTPS://GENI.US/SAVINGHERRESCUER

∽

Sensual Sounds: A Rockstar Ménage

Lust. Lies. Double lives.

. . .

THE ROCK and roll industry is full of people who are looking out for themselves and willing to do anything to rise to the top.

HTTPS://WWW.HOTANDSTEAMYROMANCE.COM/COLLECTIONS/ FRONTPAGE/PRODUCTS/SENSUAL-SOUNDS-A-ROCKSTAR-MENAGE

∽

ON THE RUN: A Secret Baby Romance

MURDER. Lies. Fraud. Just another day in the lives of billionaires and women on the run.

HTTPS://WWW.HOTANDSTEAMYROMANCE.COM/COLLECTIONS/ FRONTPAGE/PRODUCTS/ON-THE-RUN-A-SECRET-BABY-ROMANCE

∽

THE DIRTY DOCTOR'S TOUCH: A Billionaire Doctor Romance

I AM A MASTER. An elitist. I am at the top of my field, and I know what I am doing.

HTTPS://WWW.HOTANDSTEAMYROMANCE.COM/COLLECTIONS/ FRONTPAGE/PRODUCTS/THE-DIRTY-DOCTOR-S-TOUCH-A-BILLIONAIRE-DOCTOR-ROMANCE

T̲h̲e̲ H̲e̲r̲o̲ S̲h̲e̲ N̲e̲e̲d̲s̲: **A Single Daddy Next Door Romance**

H̲e̲'s **the only man I've ever wanted...**

https://www.hotandsteamyromance.com/collections/frontpage/products/the-hero-she-needs-a-single-daddy-next-door-romance

Y̲o̲u̲ c̲a̲n̲ f̲i̲n̲d̲ **all of my books here:**

H̲o̲t̲ a̲n̲d̲ S̲t̲e̲a̲m̲y̲ **Romance**
https://www.hotandsteamyromance.com

COPYRIGHT

©Copyright 2020 by Eliza Duke - All rights Reserved

In no way is it legal to reproduce, duplicate, or transmit any part of this document in either electronic means or in printed format. Recording of this publication is strictly prohibited and any storage of this document is not allowed unless with written permission from the publisher. All rights are reserved.

Respective authors own all copyrights not held by the publisher.

www.ingramcontent.com/pod-product-compliance
Lightning Source LLC
LaVergne TN
LVHW011732060526
838200LV00051B/3142